This edition published by
Reader's Digest Young Families, Inc.
Pleasantville, NY 10570
www.readersdigest.com

YOUNG FAMILIES

Reader's Digest, the Pegasus logo, and
Reader's Digest Young Families are registered trademarks of
The Reader's Digest Association, Inc.

Brave
Little Fox

Muriel Pépin
Adapted by Patricia Jensen
Illustrations by Catherine Fichaux

Reader's Digest Young Families, Inc.

When the time came for Mother Fox to have her cubs, she went looking for a home. Soon she found a roomy hollow at the bottom of a tree.

"This will be a fine place to raise my family," Mother Fox thought. "It will be warm and quiet. I am very lucky to have found it."

A few days later, just as the newborn cubs were settling down for a nap, a badger family appeared in the doorway.

"What are you doing in our home?" asked Mother Badger.

"I'm sorry," said Mother Fox. "I didn't know anyone lived here."

Mother Badger looked at the tiny sleeping fox cubs and said gently, "There's plenty of room here for all of us."

"You are very generous," said Mother Fox.

Mother Fox cared for her cubs in the cozy hollow. Soon the cubs were able to go outside on their own.

"Would you like to play with me?" Little Fox asked a young badger one day.

Little Badger nodded happily. "Sure!" he said. "I'll teach you how to play hide-and-seek!"

"Let's go!" said Little Fox.

The two young animals scampered off to play in the woods.

Little Fox and Little Badger became great friends. They tumbled in the grass and chased butterflies during the day. At night they snuggled close together in the cozy hollow. Little Fox taught his friend how to leap off tree stumps. Little Badger showed Little Fox how to dig a sturdy underground shelter.

Little Fox tried to teach Little Badger how
to catch fish in the moonlit pond. But his friend
was frightened by the dark water.

"I'm not as brave as you are," Little Badger said to Little Fox.

"I'm not always brave," Little Fox said. "I'm afraid of the eagle that flies over our house."

"So am I," said Little Badger.

One afternoon Little Badger was taking a nap when Little Fox noticed a large shadow on the ground. He looked up and saw the eagle. The powerful bird was heading straight toward them!

Little Fox began to bark loudly. "Wake up!" he called to Little Badger. "It's the eagle!"

Little Badger jumped up. The two friends ran toward home as fast as they could.

"Hurry!" shouted Little Fox.

"I can't keep up!" cried Little Badger.

Little Fox looked up at the sky. The eagle was getting ready to plunge down on them. Little Fox scrambled onto a high rock. He leaped into the air just as the eagle swooped.

"Grrr!" Little Fox growled.

The frightened eagle missed its target and was so startled that it flew away.

Little Fox expected to land on the soft grass, but instead he fell into a deep hole. His hind legs slipped between two rocks.

"Help!" he cried. He clawed the slippery ground and pulled as hard as he could. It was no use. He was stuck.

"Help!" he wailed again.

Little Badger's face suddenly appeared at the top of the hole. "Don't worry," he said confidently. "I'll get you out. Grab my tail and hold tight."

Then the strong young badger pulled his friend out of the hole.

The two little animals raced home to tell their families about their adventure.

"Little Fox was very brave," said Little Badger. "He saved us from the eagle."

"But I didn't feel brave when I was trapped in that hole," said Little Fox. "I needed you to pull me out of there."

"I think we all learned a wonderful lesson today," said Mother Fox. "Bravery comes easily when you must help someone you care about."

Little Fox and Little Badger smiled. Both were happy to have a brave and loyal friend.

The most common fox in North America has red fur and a long, bushy tail.

In the far North, foxes are camouflaged. Their fur changes from brown or gray in the summer to white in the winter, so the foxes blend in with their surroundings.

The sand fox lives in the desert. Its huge ears enable it to hear very well. It can even hear insects crawling across the sand.

Foxes hunt mainly at night. They eat rabbits, birds, small rodents, and large insects. Foxes also catch fish for food.

Farmers don't like foxes because foxes often steal grapes, honey, and chickens. But foxes also get rid of mice, which eat the farmers' crops.

The fox's main enemies are wolves, birds of prey, and humans who hunt foxes for their beautiful fur.